This book belongs to:

_____

Forbidden Talent

STORY AND ILLUSTRATIONS BY **Redwing T. Nez**

AS TOLD TO KATHRYN WILDER

Northland Publishing

Illustrations were done in oils on canvas
Text type was set in Monotype Walbaum
Display type was set in Papyrus
Designed by Trina Stahl
Edited by Stephanie Bucholz
Production supervision by Lisa Brownfield
Manufactured in Hong Kong by South Sea International Press Ltd.

FIRST IMPRESSION
ISBN 0-87358-605-0

Library of Congress Catalog Card Number 95-11087
Cataloging-in-Publication Data

Nez, Redwing T., 1960-
Forbidden talent / by Redwing T. Nez ; as told to Kathryn Wilder ;
[illustrated by Redwing T. Nez]. — 1st ed.
p.   cm.
Summary: Ashkii, who lives on an Indian reservation with his grandparents,
finds that his way of painting is in conflict with what his grandfather calls the "Navajo Way."
ISBN 0-87358-605-0
1. Navajo Indians—Juvenile fiction. [1. Navajo Indians—Fiction.
2. Indains of North America—Fiction. 3. Grandfathers—Fiction.
4. Painting—Fiction.] I. Wilder, Kathryn, 1954-   . II. Title.
PZ7.N4883Fo 1995
[Fic]—dc20   95-11087

0541/7.5M/9-95

TO THE GRANDFATHERS,

ELDERS AND MEDICINE MEN OF THE DINÉ,

FOR THEIR COURAGE.

I'm supposed to be doing my homework, but I stare into the lamplight instead. I love the way it makes the room look at night.

Grandfather has told me that it's not good for a boy like me to be thinking about painting all the time. "The Ancient Ones made too much art," he says, "and they are no longer here. Painting for fun and frolic is forbidden."

Something calls from outside. Is it Coyote? The dogs don't bark. I hear it again. Owl?

To the Diné, Owl is bringer of bad news. I turn to ask Grandfather what this could mean, Owl calling near the sheep corrals, but he is asleep in his chair.

When morning comes, my cat yawns and stretches beside me. I stretch, too. "I guess Owl's message wasn't for me," I say. "I didn't have any bad dreams."

"What?" I say, but everything outside looks the same. "Owl came and nothing bad happened. What would happen if I didn't pray?" I decide to try it.

I eat quickly. "*Ahéhee'*, thank you, Grandmother," I say, running out to get my sheep. Grandfather waves as I follow the sheep with my dog.

Walking in the direction of Owl Springs, I remember the
white clay there. "I could use the clay like paint! But what would
Grandfather say?"

Yellow Dog barks.

"How will he know?" I say. "Is that what Owl meant—that I
might get in trouble again?"

Grandfather makes sandpaintings, and he is teaching me how.

"It is the Navajo Way," Grandfather says. "It serves a purpose, and helps to keep the universe in balance." He tells me how he learned from his grandfather, who learned from his. He shows me how to make straight lines with the white, blue, yellow, and black colors he gathers from Mother Earth and mixes with sand. The colors stand for the Four Directions—East, South, West, and North.

One time I made a sandpainting for Grandfather. I worked hard, drawing things I saw in the picture books at school. But when I showed it to Grandfather, he said, "That is *not* the Navajo Way."

Grandfather told me again how prayer goes with sandpainting, how the *hataałi*, the medicine men, use it to help sick people, and how I need to follow that way or not do it at all. "Sandpainting is not playful art," he said. "It is work and prayer and beauty. It is for ceremony and healing. *Baa hasti'*—it is to be respected."

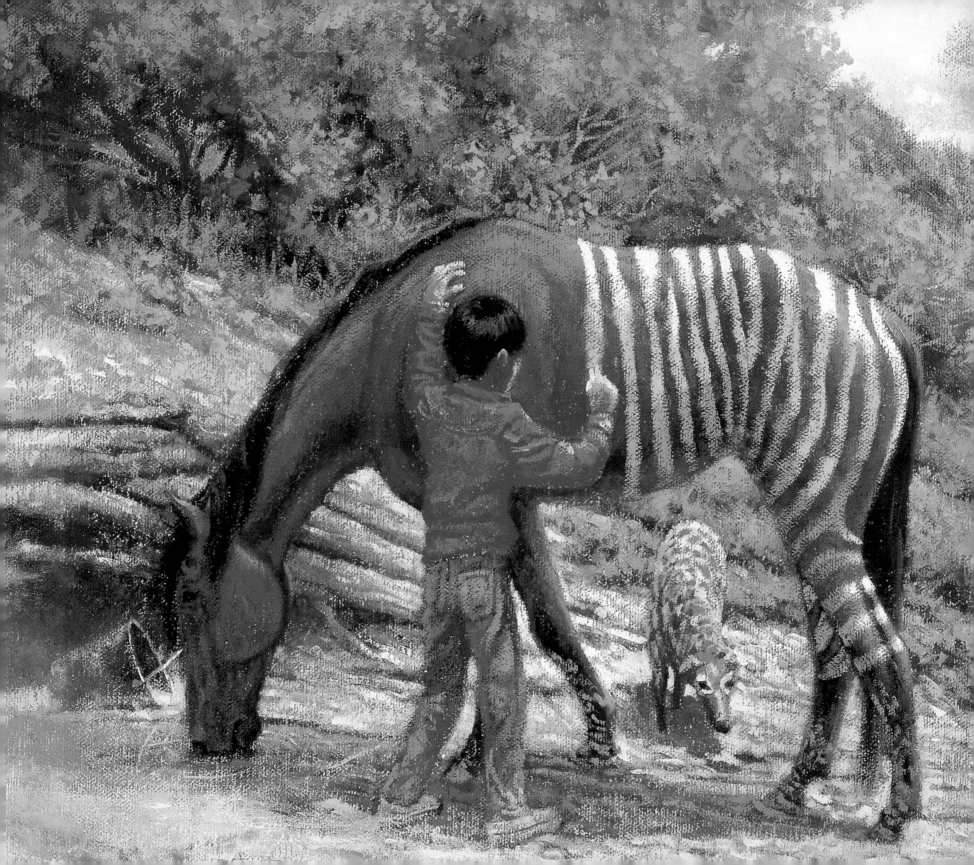

The sheep and Yellow Dog drink from Owl Springs, but I'm forbidden to. An owl drowned in here a long time ago, making the water bad.

But I heard Owl calling in the night and I didn't pray in the morning and nothing has happened. "I'm going to drink," I tell Yellow Dog.

Yellow Dog watches me. Nothing happens. "*Hágo*—Come here," I say to him, digging my fingers into the white clay. "Sit still." Pretty soon Yellow Dog is a spotted dog. Still nothing happens, so when one of the horses that lives around here comes to water, I make him a zebra.

I decide to climb up behind the spring, where the Cliff People lived—*Ánaasází*, Ancient Ones, we call them. Grandfather has told me not to go up there, because if I disturb the spirits of the Cliff People they may become angry. "It is not good to touch the things of the Ancient Ones," Grandfather says. "We leave them alone, undisturbed, out of respect." But I want to see the patterns they made on the pots. And today seems like a good day to go, since Owl called and I didn't pray and I drank the bad water and nothing has happened.

"What do you think?" I say to Yellow Dog on the way home. "*I* think Owl was wrong." Most of the white clay has flaked off Yellow Dog, but when he wags his tail more goes flying.

The next day, Grandfather and Grandmother leave for town while it is still dark. "Maybe I won't pray again today," I tell my cat. "What do you think about that?" She opens one blue eye and closes it again.

I take out my school watercolors and paint on paper and cardboard. I draw sheep and horses and dogs and my cat, who watches me. I paint her eyes the blue of the sky.

"When do you think Grandfather's coming home?" I say to her. "What would he say if he saw this?" She hits at my brush with her paw, and I hide the paintings.

Outside, the sun is already high in the sky. I run to let the sheep out. They are hungry and thirsty, but none are sick. I am not sick either, but I am confused. I do everything forbidden and nothing bad happens.

Today we will go to the spring that fills the water tank near the sheep-dipping corrals. "Remember the branding at the corrals last year?" I ask my horse. "All the neighbors had different brands and used different colors of paint." Grandfather was busy helping with a neighbor's band of sheep, so I got busy with ours. Our brand is a *J*, but I liked the way some of the others looked better. Pretty soon our sheep were the fanciest of all.

"Ashkii!" Grandfather said. "What have you done?"

"Look how they stand out," I said. "You could see ours from way over there." Grandfather's brown eyes got brighter and he walked away.

He walked away that other time, too—the time I painted his favorite horse for the Fourth of July rodeo. "Remember how pretty he looked?" I say to the horse I am riding. "Too bad Grandfather didn't think so!"

"Ashkii, you must not paint everything you see!" Grandfather said. "It will get you in trouble. The Cliff People with all their painting on pottery are no longer here." But he rode his horse that way in the parade.

At the spring by the water tank, the sheep and Yellow Dog and my horse drink for a long time. But this water isn't forbidden, and I'm not thirsty. "*Hágo*—Come here," I say to my horse when she's finished, but sometimes she doesn't respond to Navajo or English so I lead her over until she's standing next to the tank. I climb up on her; she doesn't move.

The tank is painted a shiny silver, and underneath it is rusty metal. I take a sharp rock and chip at the paint. "Look!" I say. I make designs on the tank the way the Ancient Ones made drawings on rocks.

After I have covered most of the tank with drawings, I realize that they will not flake off like the white clay at Owl Springs, or be hidden like the paintings in the cabin. "Uh-oh," I say. "Everybody who brings their sheep here to water will know. Even Grandfather!"

When I catch up with my sheep, I look back at my artwork. Even though I know I have to tell Grandfather before somebody else does, I like what I see.

The next day is a school day, and I have to wait to talk to Grandfather. I run home after school. Everything is quiet. The sheep are gone; Grandmother has taken them out today. I don't see or hear Grandfather anywhere, and I think maybe he's not home.

When I open the cabin door, sunlight falls in and lights up the inside. "Grandfather!" I say.

"Ashkii!" he says. He looks just like me.

"If painting is forbidden, Grandfather, why are you doing it?" I ask. I feel tears pushing at my throat, and I think I should have listened to Owl, after all. My cat, who was watching Grandfather paint, comes over to sit by me.

"I have something to tell you, Grandfather," I say. He pats the floor next to him. "I heard Owl calling in the night . . . "

I tell him my story about not praying and drinking water at Owl Springs and the white clay and the Cliff People's pottery and the paintings and, finally, the water tank at the sheep-dipping corrals.

"The ability to draw and paint is a gift given by the Creator," Grandfather says. "It must be used wisely, for a purpose. Maybe for healing, maybe to show others the way of our people, maybe to earn money for a family." He pulls a small leather bundle from inside his shirt. "We offer thanks for all things, even for what we don't understand. That is the Navajo Way. Today you may not understand why your talent is forbidden, but someday you will. Owl will be there to remind you to use it wisely."

Today it is still dark when I get up. My cat opens one blue eye and watches me from the bed as I put on my jacket to go outside. "Lazy," I whisper. I don't want to wake Grandfather, yet.

In the early light I see the shape of Mother Earth to the east. I think about how I will paint that someday, but right now I have something to do. I take Grandfather's leather bundle from inside my shirt. Yellow Dog leans against me in the dark as the wind scatters the cornmeal to the Four Directions. "*Ahéhee'*, thank you," I say to each.

Inside, I touch Grandfather's shoulder. "Wake up, Grandfather. Today is an important day." Grandfather and I have entered one of my paintings in an art show.

"Every day is important," Grandfather says. "This day is no different." But he dresses quickly. When we get to the show, we find a blue ribbon by my painting. Outside, I see all the colors of the rainbow, all the colors I have used in my painting, sparkling in Grandfather's eyes.

A Note on the Story

Redwing T. Nez was born in 1960 and raised on the Navajo Reservation in northeastern Arizona. His grandparents, with whom he lived for much of his childhood, had no plumbing, telephone, or electricity, so Redwing grew up without the influence of television or light bulbs. This enhanced his perception of light and color, as did his treks into the hills following the family's sheep herd.

While in government boarding school, Redwing became fascinated by the pictures he saw of famous artists and their art. What stood out most to him was that the artists had blue eyes. He thought his brown eyes were the reason he was forbidden to paint, and he considered his blue-eyed cat, as far as he knew the only one on the Reservation, sacred, and hoped her blue eyes would rub off on him.

The color of his eyes didn't change, but perhaps his blue-eyed cat did possess magic. Redwing's passion for painting continued to grow, and at twenty-two the self-taught artist discovered that people would actually pay money for his work. Now successful enough to display his award-winning artwork at the La Fonda Hotel during Santa Fe's Indian Market, Redwing still remembers where he came from, and his cat, who appears in many of the illustrations of *Forbidden Talent*.

For Redwing, creating *Forbidden Talent,* his first children's book, was not only a journey into his past but also a reminder that the spiritual basis of the Navajo Way lies in the very land that sustains the Diné. As a child not preoccupied with television, Redwing found amusement in every lava rock, juniper tree, and animal, wild or tame, he stumbled upon, and discovered some rather unconventional methods of making art. The illustrations in *Forbidden Talent,* such as that of Ashkii turning a horse into a zebra with white clay, were created from Redwing's memory. His middle child, Aukee Jake Nez, who is seven and an artist himself, posed for the paintings, and Redwing searched through old boxes to find "props" that would take him back in time.

Redwing and I hiked to the cliffs overlooking the place of his childhood, and bounced over dirt roads in a pickup truck to his grandparents' cabin, Owl Springs, and what remains of the sheep-dipping corrals. Looking out over miles of rugged Reservation land, Redwing pointed and told stories. "See that draw behind those cliffs? I used to hide my horse in there, and pretend I was hiding stolen horses from the army. Then I would climb up and parachute rocks over the edge, until I saw that my sheep were too far away."

To create the historical paintings that are his current obsession, Redwing has to revisit the past over and over again in just such a way. His experience as a Sioux warrior in Kevin Costner's *Dances With Wolves* has helped him to do so. "When I get ready to paint," he told Lois Jacka, author of *Enduring Traditions: Art of the Navajo,* "I have to go back into it again in my mind—the dust, the noise, the buffalo, the thrill. That's what excites you in painting—the feeling. It must be in the soul before it can come out in art."

Redwing's soul, like that of the Diné, lies in the crevasses between rocks, in sheep herds roaming up canyons toward water, in the rays of the sun parting salmon clouds at twilight, and in the teachings of grandfather to grandson. Redwing dedicates this book to the grandfathers, elders, and medicine men of his people, for their courage. They let generations of Navajo youth go off the Reservation to government boarding schools, holding only faith that some would return. Redwing was one of those. He lives on the Reservation, and he lives the Navajo Way. And through his ceremonial practices and his art work, the Navajo Way lives in him.

—KATHRYN WILDER

About the Authors and Illustrator

Photograph courtesy of John Running.

Self-taught artist **Redwing T. Nez** was born on the Navajo Reservation in northeastern Arizona in 1960. At twenty-two, he went to his first Indian Market in Santa Fe, New Mexico, with a car full of oil paintings and a pocket full of just enough money for gas. Two days later, he returned home a professional artist.

Although *Forbidden Talent* is Redwing's debut as author-illustrator of a children's book, his award-winning artwork has been widely collected. His work and words appear in Northland's *Enduring Traditions: Art of the Navajo,* which was the 1994 Indian Market featured book, and his various activities in the entertainment industry include an appearance in the film *Dances With Wolves.* Redwing has three sons: Lukai, Aukee, and Eli (pictured at left). He lives on the Reservation, where he can climb the cliff behind the house he grew up in and see his whole life "right [there] in this valley, in [those] rocks." That life can be seen in his traditional and contemporary paintings, as well.

Kathryn Wilder edited the highly acclaimed fiction anthology, *Walking the Twilight: Women Writers of the Southwest,* a Northland book.